AF491503

NEVER
ENDING
SIESTA
STAY HOME
STAY SAFE

<u>AUTHOR</u>

AISHWARYA K

<u>ILLUSTRATION BY</u>

AVINASH

NEVER
ENDING
SIESTA
STAY HOME
STAY SAFE

Stuck at home, due to lockdown and COVID-19, As humans we face too much frustrations and mood swings. Sometimes we feel scared, women at home feel the pressure and workload and kids may enjoy the holidays.

What about our pets, ever wonder what our pet animals are feeling? Do we humans care for them? Mean time we had rumors that pets may spread Corona. After hearing all these what is our pet thinking.

This story does not mean to hurt anyone feeling. Just an imaginary thought about pets during COVID-19.

"The Protagonist of our story is Dolby a pet.
Life during COVID-19 Dolby perspective."

Hi, Am Dolby, your friend. My family includes Dad, mom, my brother Raj and My baby sister Neena.
Neena and I are of same age. We share birthday on same day. Mom use to make single cakes for both of us and will make wish blow single candle and we lived a happy life.

Every day Dad will go to work, and Raj will go to school.
Mom takes care of me and Neena at home.

Mom gave me food and takes me for walk. Used to play with Dad and Raj in the evening.

During night I go to sleep in my house while everyone else will sleep in their respective rooms. Dad has made separate comfy little home for me to sleep peacefully at night.

Life was moving happily ever after. One fine day Dad came early from office.

He was enquiring to Mom about something. The following day Dad and Raj were staying at home.

They did not go for work or school. My day continued as usual. But mom did not take me for walk she told me it is not safe to go outside, and she gave me an affectionate pat.

I stayed at home and happily played with Raj and Neena.

I saw Dad and Mom discussing about something serious.
Some danger has hit the world, they called it a **virus**.

Which can kill humans. I felt sad. I wanted my family to be safe. My family was safely staying at home. To make sure everything is fine I stayed near the main door so no virus can come in and none at home will go out.

Dad and mom happily said look our Dolby is guarding us. Proud moment indeed.

Dad gave me a hug and Neena gave me a sweet kiss. I felt Happiest whole world.

As days passed dad started working from home and Raj studying from home. They all enquired about their near and dear through phone. My dearest people were with me, so I did not care to contact anyone. Life felt good, though the tension about the virus was increasing and dead tolls raised day by day.

I was selfish I only cared too much about my family and I did not care about anyone else. May be that's reason God punished me.

The disaster day of my life which should not have happened.

Usual morning Dad was getting ready to buy essentials for home. He was well prepared to go out. He wears his mask safely carry his hand sanitizer and when he reached home, mom used to wash all essentials well and dad used to take a bath if necessary.

Everything was fine, dad gave me and Raj a hug and he went out. Mom was busy in the kitchen and Neena was sleeping. Raj said Dolby let us play hide and seek. Mom told us not to go outside and only play around premises of house. I was naughty boy I never listen to Mom. But mom never scolds or beat she always gave me treats if am good boy.

So, this time also I did not listen to her. I went out of house and saw a small truck parked near the house and went inside the truck and hide there so Raj can never find me.

Raj was searching for me everywhere but could not find me.

He sat near the main door and he was shouting Dolby come out I lost.

I like to win hide and seek
games. So, I was about to
leave the truck suddenly I
felt truck moving.
Before I could leap outside it
started moving in a high
speed. I shouted and
shouted but no one heard
my voice. I got scared,
where are they taking me?
Am I lost? I want to go
home. Raj save me, I cried
out loud.

After about an hour or two. The truck stops at a location and it was dark, I could not see a thing. All I could see were tall buildings. I did not dare to step out of the truck what if truck again parks near my house.

I can go back home. I felt
sad, I was hungry and tired.
I slept of tiredness. I felt
something entering me.
Some form of light struck
me.

The next day, the same place. I saw someone opening the truck door. It was dad. He came searching for me. Happy tears, I went jumping into my dad's arms. Heeeey!!! Dolby are you scared he asked and gave me a hug. Dad took me home, I felt happy to again see Mom, Raj and Neena. I promised mom that I will be a good boy and never go outside house again.

I felt happy to be back home. Days went happily like this. I was constantly thinking about the light which entered inside me. After few days I felt Ill.

But I did not care much and as usual played with Raj. Sudden I collapsed, Raj got scared he shouted mom, dad come quickly Dolby is sick.
The last memory I had was seeing mom coming running to me. Then I fainted.

They took me to
hospital, when I
woke up, I was
surrounded by
unknown faces, I
got really scared
and I started
shouting.

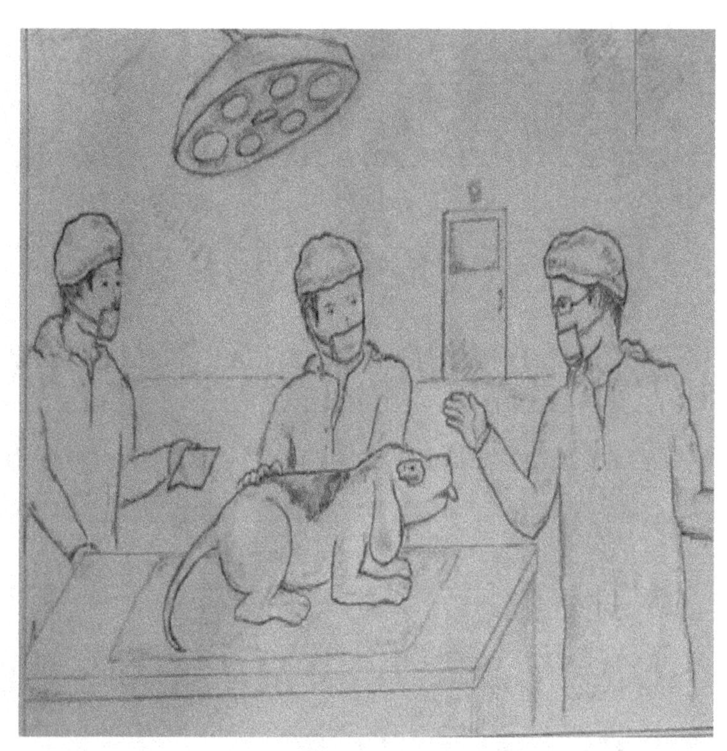

Sudden I heard a familiar
voice it was my doctor uncle.
Mom use to take me to
doctor uncle for regular
check-ups felt a quick relief.

Hey there Dolby, how are you buddy? Dr. Uncle asked me and gave me a pat. He was also wearing a mask just like dad. He told me not to worry and I will be home soon, but he was lying to me.

The light which stuck me was the virus which kill people. I too became a victim of that disease.

Days passed, I was under treatment, only known face was Dr. Uncle, he continued to give me false hope that I will be home soon.

He had personal care for me so he video called to Mom and I saw my family once again. They were sad, they missed me so much. Mom was crying. Neena was calling my name Dolby Dolby.

I felt the pain which no medicine can cure. My health condition was improving. I was winning over the virus, today am waiting for my final test result so I can go home.

I was filled with full of thoughts about happy moments I had with my family. Suddenly I felt little uneasy and I fainted...... The last vision I had was the days I happily spent with my family.

The virus was slowly eating me up, I did not have any symptoms, but I lost the battle and left my loved ones for ever. I always loved to take naps; Now took a long nap which will never end. **THE NEVER-ENDING SIESTA(NAP).**

Today my family is mourning for my lose.

—

- DOLBYs REQUEST TO ALL

- # STAYHOME

- # STAY SAFE

- #YOUR FAMILY AND LOVED ONCE NEED YOU

B'END